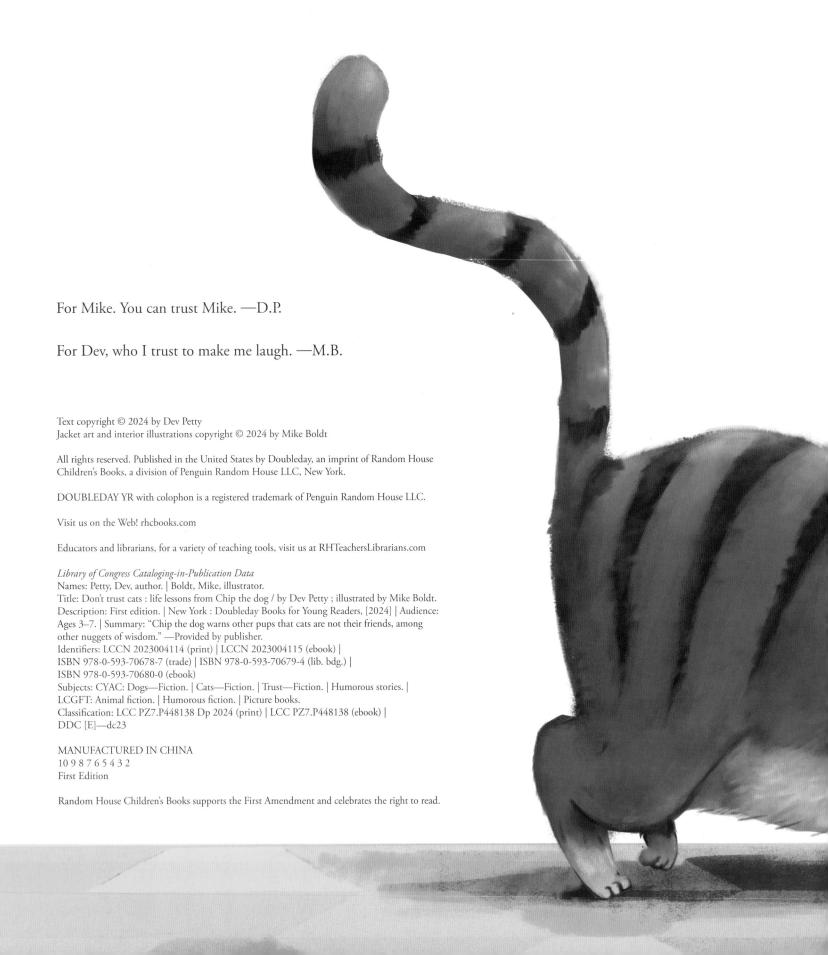

For Mike. You can trust Mike. —D.P.

For Dev, who I trust to make me laugh. —M.B.

Text copyright © 2024 by Dev Petty
Jacket art and interior illustrations copyright © 2024 by Mike Boldt

All rights reserved. Published in the United States by Doubleday, an imprint of Random House Children's Books, a division of Penguin Random House LLC, New York.

DOUBLEDAY YR with colophon is a registered trademark of Penguin Random House LLC.

Visit us on the Web! rhcbooks.com

Educators and librarians, for a variety of teaching tools, visit us at RHTeachersLibrarians.com

Library of Congress Cataloging-in-Publication Data
Names: Petty, Dev, author. | Boldt, Mike, illustrator.
Title: Don't trust cats : life lessons from Chip the dog / by Dev Petty ; illustrated by Mike Boldt.
Description: First edition. | New York : Doubleday Books for Young Readers, [2024] | Audience: Ages 3–7. | Summary: "Chip the dog warns other pups that cats are not their friends, among other nuggets of wisdom." —Provided by publisher.
Identifiers: LCCN 2023004114 (print) | LCCN 2023004115 (ebook) |
ISBN 978-0-593-70678-7 (trade) | ISBN 978-0-593-70679-4 (lib. bdg.) |
ISBN 978-0-593-70680-0 (ebook)
Subjects: CYAC: Dogs—Fiction. | Cats—Fiction. | Trust—Fiction. | Humorous stories. |
LCGFT: Animal fiction. | Humorous fiction. | Picture books.
Classification: LCC PZ7.P448138 Dp 2024 (print) | LCC PZ7.P448138 (ebook) |
DDC [E]—dc23

MANUFACTURED IN CHINA
10 9 8 7 6 5 4 3 2
First Edition

Don't Trust Cats

(Life Lessons from Chip the Dog)

written by
Dev Petty

illustrated by **Mike Boldt**

DOUBLEDAY BOOKS FOR YOUNG READERS

Chip here. I have been described as very smart and also a dog.

You're probably thinking, "Hey, Chip, I am also a dog. You seem incredibly intelligent. How can I be my best dog self?"

Great question, and because I am a good boy, I will answer.

Three words...

Don't trust cats!

Not the fluffy ones _or_ the stripy ones _or_ the very tiny ones with big eyes, no matter how adorable they are. If it has a ball of yarn, walk away.

Don't be sad. There are many things you _can_ trust.

If you're looking for animal companionship, trust this friendly-looking fella.
I have a really good feeling about this.

Those birds and squirrels you try so hard to catch? You can trust them. They're laughing <u>with</u> you, not at you.

However...
definitely avoid **bees** (long story).

And don't trust cats!

Trust your persons...
even if they aren't grateful
when you give
yourself a bath...

and they throw away the wonderful gifts you bring them,

again...

and again.

And even though they said you were going to the park that one time but it wasn't the park at all.

And sure, he cheats at cards, but you <u>can</u> trust Grandpa. He's the one who looks in your eyes and says you're a good dog and a pretty dog and keeps those special treats shaped like bones just for you.

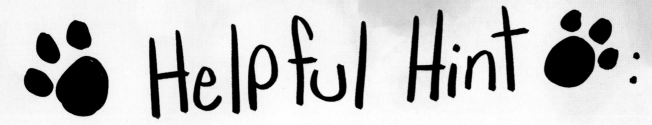 # Helpful Hint :

The small persons will show
their affection in confusing ways.

Try to be polite.

Persons are way
better than cats.

The park is full of trustastic things. You can trust that your persons will be happy when you "do" your business. They are SO proud, they even collect it and put it in a protective wrapper.

Trust this fire hydrant. It's always been there for you.

Trust your intuition about others.

This guy here loves sharing.

Trust your nose. It will lead you to *magical* things you can bring to your persons. They will be <u>SO</u> pleased.

Trust that any bed can be comfortable if it's the right bed.

You just have to be motivated.

Keep walking, Mittens.

Don't
trust the vacuum

or cactuses.

Or those two **Criminals** at the door.

But all these things are better than trusting cats. Which you should never, ever do.

Unless they seem very, **VERY** sorry... and they share their special treats with you. Well, then maybe you can trust them just a little.

Besides, you never know when a cat will do something nice, like introducing you to some new friends!